To:
From:

To my wife, Jill, a devoted teacher who tirelessly pours herself into every student. —GL

For Mae DeBruyn: Your writing workshop classes at TBCS are what got me here! —CM

For all the dedicated teachers in the world, especially my sister Emma. —LA

Discover other books in the series!

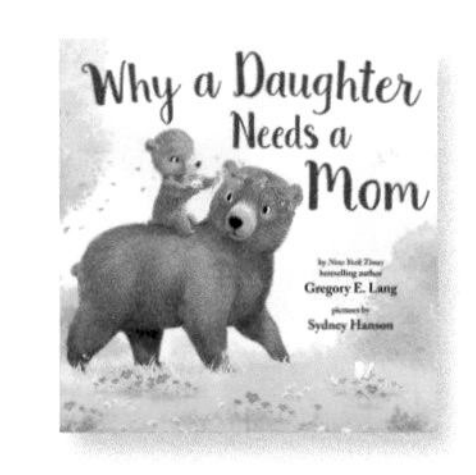

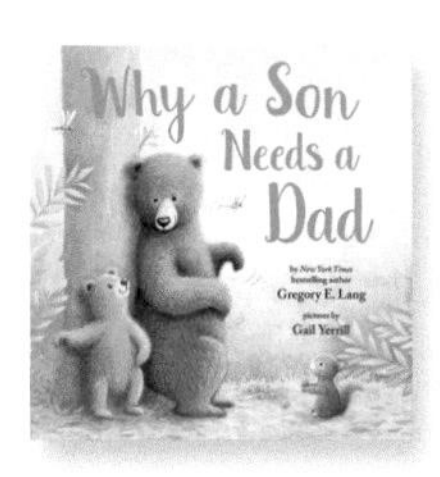

Text adapted for picture book by Craig Manning

Illustrations by Lisa Alderson

The full color art was prepared using mixed media.

Published by Sourcebooks Wonderland, an imprint of Sourcebooks Kids

P.O. Box 4410, Naperville, Illinois 60567-4410

(630) 961-3900

sourcebookskids.com

Cataloging-in-Publication Data is on file with the Library of Congress.

Source of Production: Wing King Tong Paper Products Co. Ltd., Shenzhen, Guangdong Province, China

Date of Production: October 2022

Run Number: 5028377

Printed and bound in China.

WKT 10 9 8 7 6 5 4 3 2 1

Why We Need Teachers

by Gregory E. Lang pictures by Lisa Alderson

Adapted for picture book by Craig Manning

sourcebooks wonderland

Who changes the world one day at a time?

Taking the pieces and making them rhyme?

Who gives us the tools to face the hard climbs?

The teachers we see every day!

Think of the things that you know how to do:

To add and subtract—and multiply too!

To read and to write, or tie your own shoe!

Well, how did you learn all those things?

Somebody taught you the numbers and words,

and the difference between a fish and a bird!

Someone taught you to count first, second, and third.

Do you know who that was? A teacher!

Teachers give us tools to make sense of things,

like how birds can fly just by flapping their wings,

or how cold, dark winters can fade into springs.

They're the key to unlocking the world.

Some days in the classroom are bound to be tough.

(And if we're being honest, long division is rough.)

But teachers will help you get through the hard stuff!

They know how to make hard things easy.

1 2 3

Because teachers turn lightbulbs on in your mind,

even when you think you're falling behind.

They give you the space and the safety to find

the things that you love and you're great at.

And it's not just in math, science, English, or art,

because learning's not simply about being smart.

Teachers help mold our brains, but also our hearts!

With their lessons on how to be kind.

Those lessons will guide you for all of your days,

every year, every grade, every growth spurt or phase.

Because caring for others, that matters always!

And can make the whole world that much better.

Moose Antlers
Teacher
Junior

Teachers push us to walk in our neighbor's shoes,

whether by helping a friend or reading the news.

They show us the world from a new set of views.

Teachers show us to care for each other!

Good teachers are people who always know how

to take things we find boring and make us think "Wow!"

"I didn't know that!" Or "Tell me more, now!"

They know how to make learning fun.

Great projects, great artwork, great stories, and more:

All greatness starts somewhere, with an idea (or four!)

And teachers can help you to open the door,

to bring your ideas to life.

One thing about people: we repeat what we see.

So, thank goodness for teachers! We all can agree:

They set the example of how we should be!

They're role models for all that we do.

Because of their knack for helping us grow,

teachers are the best guides to a better tomorrow!

Every doctor, or artist, or world leader you know,

started in a classroom with their teacher, like you!

And teachers aren't just the adults at your school!

They're the coaches in sports who show you the rules,

or the people who train you to swim in a pool,

because teaching can take many forms.

Teachers give us so much, and ask little in return,

except maybe the privilege of watching us learn!

So maybe it's time, perhaps it's their turn,

to be told just how much we need them.

Next time you see your teachers, say "thank you."

And tell them they matter, because we all know that's true!

Someday you'll look back and know how much you grew

all thanks to the teachers who shaped you.